THE SEATTLE PUZZLE

created by
GERTRUDE CHANDLER WARNER

Illustrated by Robert Papp

ALBERT WHITMAN & Company
Morton Grove, Illinois

The Seattle Puzzle
created by Gertrude Chandler Warner;
illustrated by Robert Papp.

978-0-8075-5560-6 (hardcover)
978-0-8075-5561-3 (paperback)

Contents

CHAPTER   PAGE

1. The Emerald City   1
2. A Mysterious Riddle   15
3. The Flying Saucer   22
4. Sniffing Out Clues   34
5. The Underground Tour   42
6. Another Look-Alike   53
7. Who Is Rachel?   60
8. In Search of a Troll   70
9. Something Fishy   81
10. Surprise!   96

THE SEATTLE PUZZLE

CHAPTER 1

The Emerald City

"Is it true, Grandfather?" asked six-year-old Benny. "Is there really an underground city in Seattle?" He couldn't believe his ears.

James Alden smiled at his youngest grandchild. "There sure is," he said, looking around the airport. "In fact, you can take a tour and check it out for yourself."

"We'll put it at the top of our list of places to see, Benny," promised Jessie, who was twelve. She often acted like a mother to her younger brother and sister.

"Don't forget," added ten-year-old Violet, "we'll be here for a whole week. That's plenty of time to see *all* the sights. Right, Henry?"

"Right," said Henry. Then he quickly added, "At least we can see quite a few." Henry was fourteen. He was the oldest of the Aldens.

Henry, Jessie, Violet, and Benny had been invited along on their grandfather's business trip to Seattle. Now they were waiting for his good friend Finn Evans to meet them.

"One thing's for sure," added Violet, "we'll be too busy sightseeing to solve any mysteries on this trip."

Grandfather chuckled. "You never know," he said. "You might be able to solve a mystery *and* see the sights at the same time."

Henry laughed. "We're good detectives, Grandfather. But we're not *that* good!" The Aldens loved mysteries, and together they'd managed to solve quite a few.

Just then, Grandfather waved as a tall man with a mustache hurried through the crowd towards them. A young woman followed quickly on his heels.

"James!" The tall man held out a hand. "I hope you haven't been waiting long. I'm afraid we got stuck in traffic."

"You couldn't have timed it better," Grandfather said, as he shook hands with Finn. "Our plane was a bit late getting in."

"This is my daughter, Reena." Finn beamed proudly as he introduced the young woman by his side. "She decided to come along for the ride."

Grandfather shook hands with Reena. Then he introduced Henry, Jessie, Violet, and Benny.

"Welcome to Seattle," said Reena with a warm smile. She was wearing a pale yellow sundress and sandals. Her wavy brown hair was pulled back into a ponytail.

"It's nice to meet you both," said Jessie, speaking for them all.

"We can't wait to see all the sights," Henry added, as Finn and Reena led the way through the crowded airport.

Inside the parking garage, Reena remarked, "You're going to love the Emerald City!"

"The Emerald City?" echoed Benny, his eyes wide. "Isn't that where the Wizard of Oz lives?"

"It's also the nickname for Seattle, Benny," Henry told him.

Grandfather nodded. "Seattle gets so much rain that everything stays green," he explained, while he helped Finn load the suitcases into the trunk of his car.

"Oh, I get it," said Benny. "And emeralds are green. Right?"

"Right!" said Reena. "You catch on fast, Benny."

"They say folks around here don't tan," said Finn. "They rust!" Everybody burst out laughing.

Jessie quickly added, "Besides, we brought along our umbrellas."

When they were settled in the car, Jessie asked, "Do you work in your father's office, Reena?"

"No, I'm afraid I don't have a head for business, Jessie. I'm studying to become a veterinarian."

The youngest Alden looked puzzled. "What's that?"

"A veterinarian is an animal doctor," Henry explained.

"Oh!" Benny nodded approvingly. "Well, guess what? We have an animal. He's a dog. We found him when we were living in the boxcar."

Reena smiled. "Oh, really? I didn't know you had a dog. But I *did* hear all about your days in the boxcar. Sounds like quite an adventure."

After their parents died, the four Alden children had run away. For a while, their home was an old boxcar in the woods. But then their grandfather, James Alden, had found them. He brought his grandchildren to live with him in his big white house in Connecticut. Even the boxcar was given a special place in the backyard. The children often used it as a clubhouse.

"I love dogs," said Reena. "I wish Watch had come along."

Jessie was surprised by Reena's words. How did she know Watch's name?

"Watch is at home," said Benny. "He's keeping Mrs. McGregor company."

"Mrs. McGregor is our housekeeper," explained Violet.

"And a super cook," added Benny. "Sometimes I even have second helpings."

"Oh, Benny!" Henry laughed. "You *always* have seconds!" The youngest Alden was known for his appetite.

As they drove into the city, Grandfather said, "One thing's for sure, you won't go hungry on this trip, Benny."

Finn was quick to agree. "Yes, we have some wonderful restaurants in Seattle."

"That reminds me of something," said Reena. "I was hoping I could take you out to lunch tomorrow. Maybe show you some of the sights. How does that sound?"

"That sounds wonderful!" said Jessie. "Are you sure it won't be too much trouble?"

"No trouble at all," Reena assured her. "I work at a pet store, but tomorrow's my day off."

"Is that all right with you, Grandfather?" asked Violet.

Grandfather gave his youngest granddaughter the thumbs-up sign. "That'll work out just fine," he told her. "I'll be tied up with business most of the day."

"Here we are!" Finn announced, as the car slowed to a stop outside the hotel.

Everyone scrambled out. Henry helped Finn unload the suitcases from the trunk.

As they stepped inside the hotel lobby, a young man in a blue blazer smiled at them from behind the front desk.

"You must be the Aldens," he said, looking at his guest list.

"That's us!" Benny piped up. "We're staying for a whole week."

"Glad to hear it! If you need anything, just ask for Toby Spinner." He pointed to the nametag pinned to his blazer. "That's me."

The youngest Alden grinned. "Hi, Toby.

I'm Benny, and this is Henry, Jessie, and Violet." He pointed to his brother and sisters. "We're going sightseeing tomorrow."

As Grandfather checked in, Toby said, "You're welcome to use the indoor pool anytime. Oh, and here are a few brochures you might find helpful. They list all the tourist attractions." He placed a handful on the counter. "And how about a few maps? We wouldn't want you getting lost."

Grandfather chuckled. "Not much chance of that," he said. "My grandchildren know how to take care of themselves."

"Jessie always gets us where we're going," Violet said, a note of pride in her voice. "She's the best map-reader in the family."

"I help, too!" put in Benny.

"You sure do," said Jessie. "We count on your sharp eyes, Benny." The youngest Alden had a way of seeing things the others didn't.

"Well, if you need anything, just let me know," said Toby. "I'm new on the job, so I'm still learning the ropes. But if I can't answer your questions, I'll find someone who can."

"Thanks, Toby," said Henry, speaking for them all.

"We'll leave you to get settled in," Finn told Grandfather.

"I'll see you kids tomorrow," added Reena. "Why don't we meet at the Hungry Heart Diner around noon, rain or shine. It's just down the street. You can't miss it."

"We'll be there!" Henry promised.

While the Aldens waited for the elevator, Jessie suddenly remembered the brochures and the maps. As she hurried back to get them, she noticed Reena deep in conversation with Toby.

Jessie didn't mean to eavesdrop, but she couldn't help overhearing.

"If they find out something fishy's going on," Reena was saying, "it'll ruin everything."

"Don't worry," said Toby. "You can count on me."

As Jessie stepped up to the counter, Reena

looked startled, as if she'd been caught doing something wrong.

"Oh!" Reena smiled uneasily. "I was, um, just...asking about the weather forecast," she said. "For tomorrow, I mean." She seemed unable to look Jessie in the eye. "Anyway, I'd better dash!" Then she hurried away.

As Jessie headed back to the elevator, she wondered just what Reena and Toby Spinner were up to.

* * * * *

Upstairs, Jessie soon forgot all about the strange conversation as she looked around their three-bedroom suite.

"Henry and Benny can share one room," she said. "Violet and I can share another, and there's one for Grandfather."

"We even have a kitchen!" Benny opened the refrigerator. "We can do our own cooking. Now all we need is food."

"Don't worry, Benny," said Grandfather. "We'll eat in the hotel restaurant tonight. Then tomorrow we'll stock up on groceries."

"We'll go shopping in the morning while you're at your meeting, Grandfather," Jessie said. "We're not meeting Reena until noon."

"Guess what?" said Violet, who was standing at the window. "We have a view of the water!"

"That's Puget Sound," said Grandfather. "It's an inlet from the Pacific Ocean."

"And look at the mountains—how pretty!" said Violet. She always noticed beautiful things.

"There's so much to see in this city," said Henry. He was sitting on the couch, the brochures spread out around him.

While Grandfather had a nap, the four Alden children looked through the brochures. "It's hard to know where to start," said Violet.

"We're starting at the Hungry Stomach Diner," said Benny. "Remember?"

Violet couldn't help smiling. "The Hungry *Heart* Diner."

"The Hungry *Heart*?" echoed Benny.

Violet nodded.

"I think the *Hungry Stomach* is a better name for a diner," Benny said after a moment's thought. "If I had a restaurant, guess what I'd call it."

"The Hollow Leg?" said Henry, a teasing twinkle in his eye.

Benny shook his head. "The Hungry Benny's Diner," he said. Everyone laughed.

"I wonder where we'll be going after lunch," said Violet.

"There's no way of knowing for sure." Henry shrugged. "It's a mystery."

"That's not the only mystery," Jessie told them.

This got Benny's attention. "What do you mean, Jessie?"

"Well, it was a bit odd," said Jessie. "Reena knew Watch's name. Did you notice?"

"What's strange about that, Jessie?" Violet wanted to know.

"How did she know it?" answered Jessie. "She said she didn't know we even had a dog."

Henry, Violet, and Benny had thought nothing of it. But now they wondered, too.

Henry frowned. "I wonder why she would lie about something like that?"

"Maybe she just made a very good guess," suggested Benny.

"Maybe," said Jessie. But she couldn't shake the feeling that something wasn't quite right.

CHAPTER 2

A Mysterious Riddle

By the time Henry, Jessie, Violet, and Benny got back from the grocery store the next morning, it was just starting to rain.

"I hope Reena still wants to go sightseeing," said Benny, while they put the groceries away.

"Remember what she said, Benny?" Violet put the onions and green peppers into the refrigerator. "Rain or shine!"

Henry pulled a jar of tomato sauce out of the grocery bag. "It's supposed to clear up," he said. "At least, that's what they said on the radio."

"Even if it doesn't, we're not going to let a little rain stop us, are we?" asked Jessie.

"No way!" cried Benny. "Nothing stops the Aldens!"

It wasn't long before they were splashing their way along the wet sidewalks. When they were almost at the diner, a woman came rushing out, hidden beneath a blue umbrella. She was in such a hurry, she almost knocked Violet over.

"Are you okay, Violet?" asked Henry. They watched the woman dash away.

Violet nodded slowly, her eyes still fixed on the woman under the blue umbrella. "I think so."

"That lady wasn't very nice," said Benny, as they stepped inside the Hungry Heart Diner.

"No, she wasn't," Jessie was quick to agree. "She didn't even stop to apologize."

The Aldens left their drippy umbrellas in a stand by the door, then made their way to an empty table by the window. No sooner had they sat down than the waitress hurried over, shaking her head.

"This section's closed, kids," she said. "If you'll follow me, there's a spot over here."

"No problem," Jessie said. They headed for an empty booth nearby.

Henry craned his neck as he glanced around. "I don't see Reena anywhere," he said. "Do you?"

Jessie shook her head. "No, but I think we're a bit early. What time do you have, Violet?"

Violet didn't answer. She seemed to be deep in thought.

"What's wrong, Violet?" Jessie asked, giving her sister a gentle nudge. She could see that something was troubling her.

"Nothing really," said Violet. "I was just thinking about that woman outside."

"The one who bumped into you?" asked Henry.

Violet nodded. "For a second, I thought it was Aunt Jane."

The others looked at her in surprise. "Aunt Jane's back in Connecticut," Henry reminded her. "Miles and miles away." Aunt Jane and Uncle Andy lived in the small town of Elmford. The four Alden children often took the bus from Greenfield to visit them.

"Besides," added Jessie, "Aunt Jane would never be that rude."

Benny was quick to agree. "She'd never bump into somebody and then just hurry away without even saying she was sorry."

"I know." Violet laughed a little. "That's what makes it so weird."

"We might as well take a look at the selections while we're waiting," Henry suggested. He reached for the menus tucked behind the shiny napkin dispenser.

"Good idea!" said Benny scooting closer to the table. "I wonder if they have any—oh!"

"What is it, Benny?" Jessie asked.

"There's a piece of paper stuck to the bottom of the table," he answered in surprise.

"Maybe it's a list of the specials," joked Jessie.

"It's a note!" said Benny, prying the folded piece of paper loose. "Can you read it, Jessie?"

Taking the note, Jessie began to read silently. Then her eyes widened and she gasped.

Violet asked, "What does it say?"

"It...it's some kind of message," Jessie said in a quiet voice.

The others were instantly curious. "Read it, Jessie," urged Benny.

"All right." Jessie nodded. Then she read aloud:

> *Through the eye of a needle*
> *a clue can be found*
> *where a saucer is resting*
> *high off the ground.*

"That sure isn't a list of the specials!" noted Benny.

Violet laughed. "We were close, Benny," she said. "It's a mystery, and that's *our* specialty."

"It doesn't make any sense," said Henry. when Jessie passed him the note. "How can

you find a clue through the eye of a needle?"

"It must be a teeny-weeny clue," Benny said. "I wonder who left the message here?"

"And why," added Jessie.

"Oh, here comes Reena!" Benny put up a hand and waved.

Jessie quickly put the note in her pocket. "Let's keep this to ourselves for now," she said in a low voice.

Nobody argued. The Aldens wanted to figure a few things out on their own first.

CHAPTER 3

The Flying Saucer

"Hi, kids!" Reena greeted them with a cheery smile. "I was afraid the rain might keep you away." She slid into the booth beside Violet.

Henry grinned. "Nothing keeps Benny away from food," he teased. Everyone laughed, including Benny.

Just then, the waitress came over to take their order. Henry chose a cheeseburger and a glass of lemonade. Jessie and Violet both had chicken strips, coleslaw, and milk.

Reena ordered a garden salad and iced tea. And Benny decided on a grilled cheese sandwich, fries, and a chocolate milkshake.

"That should do it for now," said Reena, closing her menu. She glanced at the name on the waitress's uniform. "Oh, your name's Gwen? That's one of my favorite names."

The waitress smiled a little. "It's short for Gwendolyn," she said, tucking a wisp of red hair behind her ear. With that, she quickly hurried away.

"It started with a contest, you know," Reena told them as they waited for their food to arrive. "That's how they chose Seattle's nickname."

Violet was surprised to hear this. "You mean, the Emerald City?"

"Didn't Seattle have a nickname before then?" Benny wanted to know.

"Oh, yes," said Reena. "It had several. It was known as the Queen City for a while. The problem was, other cities had the same nickname. And some people called it the Rainy City because it rains so much here."

"I like the Emerald City best," said Violet. "Don't you, Jessie?"

But Jessie wasn't listening. She was watching their waitress lead a young couple to the table by the window. "That's funny," she remarked. "I thought that section was closed."

The others glanced over. "Our waitress asked us to move over here," Violet explained to Reena.

"It probably just opened up," guessed Reena. "The lunch crowd's trickling in."

Jessie nodded. But she couldn't help noticing that there were still some empty booths.

"I'm hoping the rain will let up," said Reena, quickly changing the subject. "I want to show you a very special place."

Benny's eyes lit up. "Is it the underground city?"

"No, Benny," Reena told him. "We'll be going *up*, not down." Seeing their puzzled faces, she added, "I'm taking you to the top of the Space Needle!"

Jessie and Henry looked at each other.

Was it just a coincidence that the strange note had mentioned a needle?

"I was reading about the Space Needle in one of the brochures," Violet said. "Wasn't it built in 1962 for the World's Fair?"

"Yes—exactly," said Reena. "The view from the observation deck is amazing. At least, it is on a clear day."

"I bet the sun comes out soon," said Benny.

Sure enough, by the time they had finished lunch, the rain had stopped.

"Will it take us very long to get there?" Benny asked, as Reena led the way along the busy sidewalks. "To the Space Needle, I mean."

"Not if we take the Monorail," Reena told him with a grin.

Benny scrunched up his face. "The Monorail?"

"It's an elevated train, Benny," Henry explained. "It rides along one rail above the ground."

"Oh, I like trains!" chirped Benny.

Jessie laughed. "We all do!"

"The Monorail was also built for the World's Fair," Reena told them. "It takes people to the Space Needle."

They were soon on the Monorail speeding above the streets and past the buildings. In no time at all, they arrived at the Seattle Center. The Aldens could hardly believe their eyes when they caught sight of the Space Needle. Craning their necks, they stared up at the slender steel beams reaching into the sky, topped by a round observation deck. Henry gave a low whistle.

"Wow!" he said, astonished. "Are we really going all the way to the top?"

"We sure are," said Reena "Just as soon as I get the tickets."

"No wonder it's called the Space Needle," Benny remarked, while Reena went over to the box office. "It goes right up into space!"

Henry nodded. "It's pretty cool."

"I'm glad you brought your camera along, Violet," said Jessie. "I bet you'll get some great shots up there."

But Violet was only half-listening. She had spotted someone coming out of the elevator. Jessie saw her, too.

"Isn't that the woman who bumped into you outside the diner?" she asked Violet in surprise.

"I'm sure of it," said Violet. Then she added, "She still has her umbrella up. I guess she doesn't know it stopped raining."

Jessie nodded. "No wonder she reminds you of Aunt Jane."

"What do you mean, Jessie?"

"It's the umbrella," Jessie pointed out. "Aunt Jane has one just like it. It's always hanging from a hook in her front hall. Remember?"

Violet snapped her fingers. "Of course! A blue umbrella with yellow ducks around the rim."

"That's one mystery solved," said Jessie.

Violet soon put all thoughts of Aunt Jane aside when Reena returned with their tickets.

"Next stop—outer space!" Benny said, as

they headed towards the elevator.

The elevator zipped up towards the sky. When they stepped out onto the observation deck, the four Aldens all cried out at once, "Ohhhh!"

Reena smiled. "This is the first place I bring out-of-town guests. It's a great place to get a bird's-eye view of the city."

For a moment, the children were too amazed to speak.

"The view takes my breath away," Violet said at last.

"I had a feeling you'd enjoy it." Reena sounded pleased.

"The buildings look like Legos," Benny said.

"You're right, Benny." Henry gazed through the safety grid around the outside of the deck. "Seattle looks like a miniature city from up here."

As they made their way around the circular deck, Reena stopped to point out the sights. "Seattle's surrounded by water and mountains," she told them. "Look over

there. That's Mount Rainier in the distance."

Jessie nodded. "It's like a big snow cone."

"That's a good way to describe it, Jessie. Everything looks small from up here. See that boat heading out on the water? It's a giant car ferry," Reena told them. "It's on its way to that island out there."

"Wow," said Henry. "Look at all those big ships out there."

"Yes, there's everything from cargo ships to fishing boats on Puget Sound," said Reena. "Back in 1897, miners came to Seattle to board ships that were headed for the Klondike gold fields up north. Nowadays, tourists travel here to take cruise ships up to Alaska."

"You can really see for miles and miles," Henry remarked.

All around them, people were pointing to the sights, some peering through telescopes set up on the deck.

"Can we look through a telescope?" Benny asked Reena.

"Go right ahead, Benny," said Reena.

"That telescope over there has the best view of the city," Reena said, pointing to an open telescope on the other side of the deck.

The children walked towards the telescope as Reena walked to the other side of the deck.

"If it has the best view of the city, I wonder why no one else is using it," said Jessie.

"I have an idea," said Violet. "Why don't I take a photo of everybody?"

"Sure!" Benny was quick to agree. "Mrs. McGregor asked us to take lots of pictures."

Jessie, Henry, and Benny posed in front of the telescope, and Violet snapped a picture.

"Mrs. McGregor will think we're in a flying saucer," Benny said.

Saucer. The word reminded Jessie of the mysterious riddle. "Wait a minute!" she exclaimed. "I think that's it."

Benny blinked in surprise. "It is?"

"What are you thinking, Jessie?" Henry could tell by the look on his sister's face that she was onto something.

Jessie tugged a piece of paper from her

pocket. It was the riddle they'd found in the menu. She read it aloud once again:

"Through the eye of a needle / a clue can be found / where a saucer is resting / high off the ground." She looked around at the others. "When Benny said 'flying saucer,' it suddenly clicked. This observation deck is the answer to the riddle."

"The saucer resting high off the ground!" Violet exclaimed. "That's good detective work, Jessie!"

Henry added, "The riddle *did* mention a needle."

"And this is the Space Needle!" cried Benny, his voice rising with excitement. Then he frowned. "But what's the eye of the needle?"

Henry had an answer. "The telescope!"

"Of course!" said Jessie. "It's like an eye looking out at the city."

"Do you see anything?" Benny asked as Henry peered through the telescope. The youngest Alden was hopping from one foot to the other with excitement.

Henry shook his head. "No wonder no one was around this telescope," he said. "I can't see anything at all."

"Wait a minute!" Jessie heard something fluttering in the breeze. "There's a piece of paper taped over the end of the telescope." She pulled it off.

"That's better!" said Henry. "I've got a good view of the city now."

Jessie caught her breath as she glanced down at the paper.

"What is it, Jessie?" Violet wanted to know.

Before Jessie could answer, she spotted Reena coming back. She quickly tucked the note into her pocket.

CHAPTER 4

Sniffing Out Clues

"Hurry, Jessie!" said Benny, who never liked to be kept waiting in suspense. "Read the note, okay?" The four Alden children had just stepped into their hotel suite after saying good-bye to Reena.

"Don't worry, Benny!" Jessie laughed. "I've been itching to get a good look at it." As they sat together on the couch, she read the latest message aloud.

Beneath all the traffic
seek out the troll

guarding a message
way down below.

"A...*a troll?*" Benny looked scared. "I heard a story about a troll—and guess what? A troll is a *monster!*"

"It's also just make-believe, Benny," Violet assured him. "Trolls are only in fairy tales."

"Let's talk about it while we get dinner started," Jessie suggested, glancing at her watch.

"Grandfather mentioned getting a pizza tonight," Benny reminded her.

"Oh, that's right," Jessie recalled. "I'd forgotten all about it."

Violet had a thought. "Why don't we surprise Grandfather with a homemade pizza?"

"Homemade?" Benny frowned. "But we're not at home, Violet."

"That's just an expression, Benny," Henry explained. "It means we'll make it ourselves."

"Can we make an extra-large pizza?" Benny asked hopefully.

"Sure," said Jessie. "We'll make the pizza now, then pop it into the oven when

Grandfather gets back from his meeting."

After washing their hands, the four Alden children set to work. They discussed the mystery while they chopped and shredded and stirred.

"Where in the world will we find a troll?" Violet wondered.

"Beneath all the traffic," Jessie answered, as she stirred the sauce at the stove. "At least, that's what the riddle says."

"Wait a minute," cried Benny, rolling out the dough. "I know what's beneath all the traffic!" The youngest Alden was up to his elbows in flour.

"What's that, Benny?" asked Henry.

"The underground city."

"Oh!" Violet put a hand over her mouth is surprise. "You're right, Benny! An underground city is way down below."

Benny beamed. It was always fun figuring out clues.

Henry sounded doubtful. "A troll in an underground city?" He paused as he grated mozzarella cheese. "It seems a bit far-fetched, don't you think?"

"It's worth checking out," Benny insisted.

Violet, who was chopping onions and green peppers, looked over. "I agree."

"It was on our list of places to see," Jessie admitted, as she tasted the sauce.

"Okay, Benny," Henry said. "We'll take the underground tour tomorrow."

Benny's face lit up. "Really?"

"We promise," Jessie said, turning to her little brother. Then she giggled. "Oh, Benny! You look like you're going out trick-or-treating."

"I do?" Benny went to look at himself in the hall mirror. He had flour on the tip of his nose, on his chin, and in his hair. "Oops! How did that happen?" Benny couldn't help grinning. "I look like I just saw a ghost," he said, as he went back to rolling out the pizza dough.

The others burst out laughing. "You look like you *are* a ghost, Benny," corrected Violet.

"A ghost looking for a troll!" said Benny.

"Keep looking, Benny," Henry shot back.

Jessie turned down the heat under the pan. The sauce was bubbling nicely. "What I can't figure out," she said, "is who would leave such a weird note."

"One thing's for sure," said Benny, "somebody knows we're detectives."

Violet looked over at her younger brother. "What makes you say that, Benny?"

"Well, why else would there be a mysterious message under *our* table?"

"Good point," said Violet. "But who knows us in Seattle?"

"Only Finn and Reena," said Henry. "And I don't think they know we're detectives."

"Besides," Violet added, "we can't be sure that note was meant for us. Don't forget, we weren't even sitting at that booth at first."

This got Jessie thinking. "That's true, Violet," she said, spooning tomato sauce evenly over the dough. "That waitress—I think her name was Gwen—insisted we move over there."

"That's because we were at the wrong

table," Benny pointed out. "That section was closed, remember?"

Jessie put the empty pan in the sink. "But she let somebody else sit there."

"You think the waitress wanted us to find the riddle?" Violet questioned. "Is that what you're saying, Jessie?" She topped the sauce with layers of mushrooms, green peppers, tomatoes, and onions.

"It's possible," said Jessie.

Henry looked over at her. "That doesn't add up, Jessie. Why would she do that?"

"She'd never even met us before today," put in Benny.

"True enough," said Jessie. Then after a moment's thought, she added, "Unless..."

"Unless what?" Benny asked.

"Unless she was working with somebody else." Jessie spoke slowly as if trying to sort out her thoughts. "Somebody who made sure we'd be there. At the Hungry Heart Diner, I mean."

"You don't really believe Reena was behind this, do you, Jessie?" Violet asked.

"Well, she *did* suggest eating at the Hungry Heart Diner," Jessie pointed out.

Violet shrugged. "The diner's just down the street from the hotel."

"But Violet," said Jessie, "Reena also took us to the Space Needle."

Henry nodded as he sprinkled cheese over the pizza. "And that's where we found the second note."

"You think it's more than just a coincidence, Henry?" Benny wondered.

"I'm not sure what to think," Henry answered. "But it is a bit suspicious."

But Violet wasn't convinced. "Anybody could've put that note under our table. Even that look-alike."

Benny frowned. "Who...?"

"You're thinking about that woman with the blue umbrella. Right, Violet?" said Jessie. "The one who reminds you of Aunt Jane."

"She was coming out of the diner," Violet said. "Then we saw her getting off the elevator at the Space Needle."

"You think there's someone—who

reminds you of Aunt Jane—going around the city planting clues, Violet?" It didn't make sense to Henry.

"Maybe she wasn't planting them, Henry," Violet said. "Maybe she was looking for clues."

The others had to admit it was possible. "Well, if she was looking for clues, she didn't find them," said Benny. "We did!"

"Now, if only we could find some answers," said Henry.

"What now?" Benny asked when the pizza was ready for the oven.

"Toby mentioned an indoor pool," said Henry. "Why don't we go for a swim before Grandfather gets back for dinner?"

Everyone thought that was a great idea. As Jessie tucked the notes into a drawer, she couldn't help wondering if they would ever be able to solve such a strange mystery.

CHAPTER 5

The Underground Tour

At breakfast the next morning, James Alden had a surprise for his grandchildren. "I'll be finished early today," he told them. "I thought it might be fun to take a ferry ride across Puget Sound. Anybody interested?"

"That sounds great!" said Benny.

"I can't wait to take pictures," added Violet.

"Why don't we meet back here after lunch?" said Grandfather.

Jessie nodded as she poured syrup onto her pancakes. "That'll give us lots of time to visit Pioneer Square."

"Pioneer Square?" Benny asked.

"That's where the underground city is, Benny," Henry explained.

Grandfather helped himself to a few strips of bacon. "That whole area burned to the ground during the Great Seattle Fire of 1889."

The children turned to their grandfather in surprise. "There was a fire?" questioned Henry.

Grandfather nodded. "Apparently, a pot of glue boiled over and caught fire."

"Oh, no!" cried Violet. "Couldn't they put it out?"

"They tried, Violet," said Grandfather, passing the muffins to Jessie. "They even formed a human chain of seawater buckets, but it was no use. Back then, most of the buildings were made of wood, so—"

Henry cut in, "The flames spread quickly."

Grandfather put down his fork. "Twenty-nine city blocks were destroyed in no time,

Henry. They decided to rebuild the city using brick and stone."

Jessie nodded in understanding. "They didn't want to risk another fire."

"Exactly," said Grandfather.

"Does anybody live in the underground city, Grandfather?" Violet asked, as she got up to clear the table.

Grandfather shook his head. "No, it's only open for tours, Violet." He poured himself a cup of coffee, then sat down on the couch to read the morning paper.

After the breakfast dishes were washed, Violet remembered her camera. When she opened the closet door, she stepped back in surprise. "What in the world...?"

"What is it?" Henry asked.

They all looked in the direction Violet was gazing. Propped up in a corner of the closet was an umbrella—a blue umbrella with yellow ducks around the rim!

"Hey, that lady had an umbrella just like that," said Benny. "The lady who bumped into you, Violet."

"You'll notice," the tour guide was pointing out, "none of the buildings in Pioneer Square are made of wood. Anybody care to guess why?" he asked.

Benny piped up, "They didn't want the city to burn down again."

All eyes turned to the youngest Alden.

"Exactly!" The guide had a brush cut and a cheery smile. He looked over at Benny in surprise. "What's your name, young man?"

"Benny Alden. And this is my brother, Henry. And my sisters, Jessie and Violet."

"Well, you hit the nail right on the head, Benny! Wooden buildings were banned in Pioneer Square after the Great Seattle Fire."

As the guide led the way past the shops, he talked about the flooding in the olden days. He finished by saying, "Sometimes the dirt roads would sink under the weight of the wagons. Huge potholes would fill up with water. Once, a young boy drowned trying to cross a pothole on a raft."

"Oh!" cried Violet. "How sad."

"They decided to raise this whole area

after the fire so that it wouldn't flood." The guide opened a door onto a flight of steps. "If you'll follow me, you'll soon find yourself on the original street level. But watch your footing," he warned them. "The sidewalks can be uneven down below."

"Are there any rats down there?" a middle-aged woman asked in a quiet voice. She sounded a bit uneasy.

"I've been giving tours for a long time," the guide answered with a shake of his head, "and I haven't seen any yet."

"How about trolls?" Benny piped up, making everyone laugh.

"Haven't spotted any trolls either." The young man grinned over at the youngest Alden. "But there's a first time for everything."

The children followed the group down the steps into a shadowy underground. They made their way slowly through a maze of dark passageways, where old ground floors had become basements, and old sidewalks had become tunnels.

"It's kind of spooky down here," said Benny, staying close to Jessie.

Jessie put a comforting arm around her little brother. "It just feels like that because of the shadows," she said, as they walked under a brick archway.

"I wonder if any ghosts are wandering around down here," Benny said in a hushed voice.

"No." Henry shook his head firmly. "Ghosts don't exist, Benny." But Benny didn't look convinced.

Violet turned to look over her shoulder. She didn't really believe in ghosts, but she couldn't help shivering a little.

"It's like stepping back in time." Jessie paused to look at an old storefront. "This must have been a bank. See the vault?"

The guide told them about the early sawmills, and how the city had grown during the Klondike Gold Rush when the miners had arrived on their way north. And all the while, the four Alden children kept a lookout for trolls.

"That was a great tour," Violet said when they stepped out into the sunlight again. "But it looks like we struck out."

"I'm afraid so," Henry agreed.

Jessie glanced at her watch. "It's almost noon. Why don't we stop somewhere for lunch?" She looked over at her little brother. "How does that sound, Benny?"

But Benny's jaw had suddenly dropped. He was staring over at the totem pole.

"Benny?" said Violet. "What's—"

Before she could finish her sentence, the youngest Alden was racing full-speed along the sidewalk.

CHAPTER 6

Another Look-Alike

Benny came to a sudden stop at the totem pole. He was looking all around when the other Aldens caught up to him.

"Benny, what's gotten into you?" Jessie asked him with a frown. "You know the rules."

"We're supposed to stay together," Henry reminded his little brother.

Violet put an arm around him. "It's a big city, Benny," she said. "We don't want anyone getting lost in the crowd."

"Sorry," Benny said sheepishly. "It's just…I thought I saw someone."

"Was it Reena?" Jessie asked. Who else did they know in Seattle?

Benny shook his head. "No, it wasn't Reena," he told them. "It was Mrs. McGregor!"

"Oh, Benny!" Jessie reached out, ruffling her little brother's hair. "Mrs. McGregor's back home in Greenfield looking after Watch."

"But I saw her, Jessie!" Benny insisted. Then he frowned. "Mrs. McGregor hurried away when she saw me. I wonder why."

Jessie shook her head. "Mrs. McGregor would never try to get away from us."

"Sometimes strangers can remind us of people we know," put in Violet. "Remember yesterday? I thought I saw Aunt Jane."

"It's just another case of mistaken identity," said Jessie, as they headed for the restaurant. "Nothing more than that."

"I suppose," said Benny. Still, his big eyes kept scanning the crowds.

They stopped to wait for a light to change. "Seattle seems like a city of look-alikes. It's funny, isn't it?" said Henry.

Jessie didn't think it was strange at all. "They say everybody has a double somewhere in the world."

The youngest Alden was surprised to hear this. "You mean there's another Benny out there?"

"Well, at least somebody who looks a lot like you," answered Violet, as they stepped into a small restaurant.

"I'm not so sure," said Henry, giving his little brother a playful nudge. "I think Benny's one of a kind." No one could argue with that.

When the waitress came over, Henry ordered the special—fish and chips and a glass of lemonade. So did the others. While they waited for their food, the children turned their attention to the mystery.

"I don't get it," said Violet. "The note seemed to be leading us right to the underground city."

Benny nodded. "That's where I'd be hiding if I were a troll."

Jessie tucked her long brown hair behind her ears. "For all we know, we could be on a wild goose chase."

"What do you mean, Jessie?" Benny wanted to know.

"Maybe these riddles are just somebody's idea of a joke."

The corners of Benny's mouth turned down. "Jessie, are you saying there might not be a mystery at all?" He looked crushed.

"Could be," said Henry.

Violet bit her lip. "I really don't know what to think."

Benny did not seem very happy.

Violet felt her little brother's disappointment. "I have a hunch there's more to it than that. Someone went to a lot of trouble leaving those notes."

Violet had a point. "We can't be sure it's just a prank," Jessie had to admit.

Benny looked more cheerful. "We can't give up yet!"

"Okay, Benny," said Henry. "Maybe if we put our heads together, we can figure something out."

Jessie read the note aloud to refresh everyone's memory. *"Beneath all the traffic / seek out the troll / guarding a message / way down below."*

Benny had a thought. "Maybe we should be looking for goats."

Henry, Jessie, and Violet stared at him. They looked totally puzzled.

Then Violet snapped her fingers in sudden understanding. "Oh, you're thinking about The Three Billy Goats Gruff."

Benny nodded. "In the story, the three billy goats are trying to cross a bridge. But guess what? There's an ugly troll with one eye and a big nose who lives under the bridge."

"I remember that story," said Jessie. "When the smallest goat tries to cross, the troll threatens to gobble him up, but—"

"The goat tells him to wait for his brother who's much bigger," Henry broke in. "So the troll lets the first goat cross the bridge."

"And then the bigger goat comes along," Benny continued, "and the troll says he'll gobble *him* up. But the bigger goat tells him to wait for his brother."

"Who's much, *much* bigger," put in Violet.

"Right," said Benny. "So the troll lets him cross the bridge, too. Then, when the biggest goat comes along, he butts the troll into the water with his big horns!"

"And the goats get away!" finished Henry.

"That's a good story," said Jessie. "I'm just not sure we'll find any goats in a big city."

"Maybe not," Violet agreed. "But there *are* plenty of bridges in Seattle."

"You think the riddle is leading us to a bridge?" Jessie asked.

"Well, think about it," Violet said. "If you're under a bridge, then you're—"

"Beneath all the traffic!" cried Benny, finishing his sister's thought.

Violet nodded. "Exactly."

"I vote we look under bridges," said Benny. "I bet that's where we'll find a troll."

Jessie frowned as she studied the map. "The thing is, Seattle has so many bridges."

"We'll only be in Seattle for a few more days," added Henry. "We'll never have time to check them all out."

"Looks like we'll have to narrow it down," Jessie said, as their food arrived.

"But how?" asked Benny.

CHAPTER 7

Who Is Rachel?

The afternoon sun was getting warm by the time the Aldens got back to the hotel. Toby waved to them from behind the front desk.

"Hi, kids!" he said. "Enjoying our beautiful city?"

"We sure are." Henry returned the desk clerk's friendly smile. "We've been checking out the sights."

"Any luck?" Toby asked.

The four Aldens exchanged glances. Did

Toby know they were trying to track down clues?

Seeing the children's startled faces, the clerk added, "I, uh… I meant finding your way around. That's all I meant about—" He stopped suddenly. "By the way, your grandfather just got back. He's waiting for you upstairs."

"Thanks, Toby," Henry called back over his shoulder as they headed for the elevator.

"That was pretty strange, wasn't it?" remarked Jessie. "Toby was awfully nervous." She pressed the elevator button.

Henry nodded. He'd picked up on this, too. "He was acting as if he'd said the wrong thing."

Benny crinkled his brow. "Do you think he knows something about the mystery?"

"Toby just started a new job," Violet was quick to remind them. "That's why he was nervous. What's wrong with that?"

"Nothing," Henry said, as the elevator doors opened. "Not if that's all it was."

"Just acting nervous doesn't make him

suspicious," Violet insisted. Violet was shy, and being around a lot of people made her nervous, too.

"You're right," said Jessie. "Still, it wouldn't hurt to keep an eye on him."

As they stepped inside the hotel suite, they heard Grandfather talking on the phone in the other room.

"We have to hope for the best," he was saying. "Yes, yes, I know...everything depends on finding Rachel."

The four Alden children didn't like the sound of this. Who was Rachel? And why was she missing?

A surprised look crossed Grandfather's face as he came into the room. "Oh!" he said. "I didn't hear you come in."

"Is everything all right, Grandfather?" asked Violet.

James Alden gave his youngest granddaughter a warm smile. "What could be wrong, Violet? It's a beautiful afternoon and the ferry awaits!"

Jessie and Henry exchanged glances.

Whatever was going on, it was clear Grandfather didn't want to talk about it. But why? And who in the world was Rachel?

* * * * *

"This was a wonderful idea, Grandfather!" said Jessie.

They were standing on the deck, enjoying the warm sun on their faces and the sea breeze in their hair. They had traveled all the way to Bainbridge Island, and now they were heading back.

Grandfather looked pleased. "It's always nice to get out on the water."

"I took so many great pictures," said Violet. "I just hope they all turn out."

It wasn't long before they were following a long line of people off the ferry and onto the dock. Violet turned around to take one last picture.

"I want to get the ferry in this shot," she said.

"No problem," said Grandfather. "That'll be a nice photo to put in our—*wait!*"

"What is it, Grandfather?" asked Jessie.

James Alden hurried them along. "I'm afraid we don't have time for any more pictures."

"But—" Violet began.

"Sorry, Violet," Grandfather cut in. "But I still have a...a business call to make. I, uh...left my cell phone back at the hotel."

Jessie glanced at Henry. This was strange. She could tell by the look on his face that he was thinking the same thing she was. It wasn't like Grandfather to be forgetful.

As soon as they were back at the hotel, Grandfather went upstairs to make his phone call. Henry, Jessie, Violet, and Benny decided to head down the street to the one-hour photo shop. While Violet was waiting in line to get her film developed, Jessie caught sight of Reena Evans through the store window. But Finn's daughter wasn't alone. Walking beside her was a young woman with curly red hair. It was Gwen—the waitress from the Hungry Heart Diner!

* * * * *

"Things are getting weirder and weirder,"

said Benny, who was perched on the bed. The four Alden children were having a late-night meeting in the room that Jessie and Violet were sharing.

"You can say that again!" said Jessie. She was sitting cross-legged on the floor, the street map opened in front of her.

"I don't get it." Henry was shaking his head in disbelief. "Reena made a big point of looking at the name on the waitress's uniform," he recalled. "Why would she pretend she didn't know Gwen?"

Violet was standing by the window looking out at the city lights. "Reena's been so nice. Why would she want to fool us?"

"We all like her, Violet," said Henry. "But it *is* suspicious."

Jessie nodded. "It's beginning to look like Reena and Gwen are up to something."

"Like what, Jessie?" Violet wondered.

At this, Jessie shrugged. "I'm not sure," she said. "But what if these riddles are just a way of distracting us."

"What do you mean, Jessie?" asked Benny.

Jessie quickly told her sister and brothers about the conversation she'd overheard between Reena and Toby. "Reena was saying, 'If they find out something fishy is going on, it'll ruin everything.'"

"You really think something fishy is going on?" Violet asked. She looked at Jessie, then over at Benny and Henry. She could see they believed it was possible.

"I bet it has something to do with Rachel," said Benny. "Whoever that is."

"Well, whoever it is," put in Jessie, "she seems to be missing."

Henry nodded. "And Grandfather said everything depends on finding her."

"We can't be sure Reena has anything to do with Rachel," insisted Violet. "Or the notes." She still had a hunch Aunt Jane's look-alike was behind everything.

"You're right, Violet," Henry agreed. "We shouldn't jump to any conclusions until we have more evidence."

"So what *should* we do?" Benny wanted to know.

Jessie looked up from the map. "I guess we'll just keep following the clues."

"Easier said than done," remarked Violet.

"That's true," Jessie said, glancing down at the map. "With so many bridges, we really have our work cut out for us."

Nobody said anything for a while. Then Jessie came across something that made her eyes widen.

"I think we can narrow our search," she announced, slowly raising her gaze.

The others were instantly curious. "Don't keep us in the dark, Jessie," Henry pleaded. "What's going on?"

"Well, maybe this is just a weird coincidence," Jessie began, "but I just found Troll Avenue on the map!"

"What?" Henry blinked in surprise.

As they crowded around, Jessie pointed a finger. "It's right here in the Fremont neighborhood."

Henry studied the map closely. "You're right, Jessie," he said. "And Troll Avenue leads under the Aurora Bridge."

Violet pressed her hands against her cheeks. "I can't believe it!"

"Then…that means—" began Benny.

Henry cut in. "It means the troll must be under the Aurora Bridge!"

"Now we're getting somewhere!" Benny rubbed his hands together.

"We can't be sure," said Jessie. "But it's worth checking out."

Benny was already halfway to the door. "What are we waiting for?"

"Daylight," Henry said with a laugh. "It's late, Benny. Remember?"

Benny looked over at the darkened window. "Oh, right!"

"I vote we get a good night's sleep," Henry said in the middle of a yawn.

"Good idea," said Jessie. "Tomorrow we have a date with a troll!"

CHAPTER 8

In Search of a Troll

"Can you believe it?" Jessie couldn't help laughing. "There might really be a troll under a bridge!" She couldn't get over it.

The four children were up bright and early the next morning. They were talking about the mystery while they made breakfast.

Benny placed napkins around the table. "I wonder what message it's guarding."

"We'll find out soon," said Henry, who was standing at the stove. "We'll head over to the bridge after we eat."

70

"I wish Grandfather had joined us for breakfast," said Violet, when they sat down at the table. "He hasn't had a chance to see the photographs yet." She reached for the envelope of photos on the table. "There was one that turned out especially well."

"You mean the one of the bald eagle?" asked Henry, swallowing a mouthful of eggs. "That was my favorite."

Violet shook her head. "No, I mean the one with Benny sleeping on the ferry." She looked through the envelope. "Here it is." She held it out to Henry. "Benny looks so cute with his head on Grandfather's lap."

Henry couldn't help smiling. "You were lost in dreamland, Benny," he said. Then his eyebrows suddenly furrowed. "Take a look at the man in this photo. The one sitting at the back of the ferry."

The others pushed back their chairs and went to look over Henry's shoulder.

Jessie's eyes widened as she looked from the photo to Henry and back again. "That can't be Uncle Andy, can it?"

"Where?" Benny asked.

Jessie tapped a finger, pointing to a man in the back row. He was sitting in the shadows, reading a newspaper.

"It does look a lot like Uncle Andy," Violet had to admit.

Henry nodded. "Enough like him to be his twin brother. At least, from a distance," he quickly added.

"It *is* Uncle Andy," declared Benny. He sounded very sure.

Violet's lips curled up into a smile. "It can't be, Benny. Uncle Andy's in Connecticut."

"Besides," put in Jessie, glancing down at the photo, "it's hard to tell what this man really looks like. After all, he's half-hidden by a newspaper."

Henry shrugged. "I guess we'll have to chalk it up to another look-alike sighting."

Violet giggled as she sat down again. "I guess it was your turn to see a double, Henry."

With that, the four Alden children finished breakfast. After leaving the kitchen spick-and-span, Henry, Jessie, Violet, and Benny headed down to the lobby.

"Hi, kids!" Toby called out to them. "Where are you off to today?"

Jessie didn't want to lie, but she didn't trust the hotel clerk with the truth. "Oh, we'd thought we'd take a look around the Fremont neighborhood."

"Well, that's quite a distance to walk," Toby informed them. "It'll be easier if you hop on the bus at the corner."

"Thanks, Toby," said Henry. Then they hurried away.

The children walked towards the bus stop, past smartly dressed men and women hurrying to work. They hadn't gone far before Benny noticed a souvenir shop. He stopped to look at the display of T-shirts in the window.

"I bet you want a T-shirt with the Space Needle on it," said Jessie, reading his mind. "Right, Benny?"

Benny looked over at his oldest sister expectantly. "Do we have enough money?"

"Well, Grandfather *did* give us some extra money for souvenirs," Jessie told him.

Inside the store, Benny made a beeline for the salesclerk. "Excuse me," he said. "I was wondering if you have any T-shirts with the Space Needle on the front?"

His brother and sisters exchanged smiles. They could always count on Benny not to waste time on small talk.

"Yes, right over here." The smiling young woman held up a T-shirt. "This one should fit."

Benny beamed. "Thank you very much!"

"I really like that purple T-shirt with the ferry on it," said Violet. Purple was Violet's favorite color, and she almost always wore something purple or violet.

Jessie glanced around. There were so many T-shirts, it was hard to choose. After much thought, she chose one with the Monorail on the front.

"I think I'll get the Seattle Mariners," said Henry, who was a big baseball fan.

"I'm guessing you're from out of town,"

the salesclerk remarked as she rang up their purchases.

Violet answered shyly, "Our grandfather's here on business."

The young woman counted out the change. "And you're off to see the sights?"

Benny piped up, "We already saw the Space Needle and the underground city. Now we're checking out the troll."

The salesclerk did not seem surprised to hear this. "The Fremont Troll always gets a lot of visitors."

The Aldens all looked at each other in surprise. "You've heard of the troll?" Jessie questioned.

"Oh, of course! It's one of the most popular art pieces in Seattle. Kids love to climb all over it." The salesclerk slipped their T-shirts into a bag.

"How about that?" Henry was shaking his head in disbelief as they stepped outside. "The riddle's leading us to a sculpture."

"I can't wait to see it," said Violet, who took a great interest in art.

It wasn't long before the children were on a bus heading towards the Aurora Bridge.

"I can see the bridge up ahead!" Benny cried out. He was craning his neck and pointing out the window.

Henry pulled on the bell. As the bus slowed to a stop, the Aldens quickly got off. There was no stopping the youngest Alden. The others gave chase as Benny led the way under the bridge. They all came to a sudden stop when they caught sight of a huge concrete sculpture of a one-eyed troll.

For a few moments no one spoke. Then Violet said, "I've never seen anything like it."

"Neither have I," said Jessie.

"And look at that!" cried Benny, staring wide-eyed. "The troll's crushing a car in his hand."

"Awesome!" Henry couldn't stop shaking his head.

For a while, they put all thoughts of the mystery aside as they climbed all over the gigantic sculpture. Violet took a snapshot of Benny standing on the troll's head, and

another one of Jessie and Henry sitting on the monster's shoulder. Finally, Benny spoke up.

"I wonder where that message could be?" he said, scratching his head.

Jessie slapped her forehead with the palm of her hand. "We almost forgot why we came!"

The children began making a careful search. They circled the troll once…twice…three times looking for the message. But no luck.

Henry scratched his head. "Maybe somebody beat us to it."

"Oh, Henry!" cried Violet. "I hope not."

But sharp-eyed Benny had spotted something the others hadn't. In a flash, he crawled under the troll's hand. He came out holding a small white box tied up with a red ribbon.

"What would we do without you, Benny?" Jessie gave him a hug.

Benny beamed. "I'm pretty good at finding things."

"You sure are," agreed Henry. The Aldens

sat down together on a concrete slab.

Sure enough, they found another note inside the box. Jessie wasted no time reading it aloud.

> *"If you catch sight*
> *of fish flying high,*
> *make your way to a bank*
> *standing nearby."*

"Flying fish?" Benny wrinkled his forehead. "That's kind of weird."

Violet agreed. "It doesn't make sense."

"Nothing about this mystery makes sense!" Henry pointed out.

"It's almost as if—" Violet stopped in mid-sentence when Jessie put a finger to her lips, signaling for her brothers and sister to be quiet.

"What is it?" Henry asked in a hushed voice.

"I'm not sure," Jessie told him, glancing around uneasily. "I just have the strangest feeling we're being watched."

The Aldens all stopped and looked around. They saw a young couple taking pictures of the troll, but they didn't see anything suspicious.

Benny leaned closer to the others. "Maybe the troll has his eye on us," he whispered, half-joking.

"That troll has a hubcap for an eye, Benny," Henry pointed out, laughing a little. "I don't think he can see much."

Jessie put a comforting arm around her little brother. "I'm sure nobody's watching," she said. She didn't want him to worry. But she really wasn't sure at all.

CHAPTER 9

Something Fishy

"An ice cream cone would sure hit the spot right now," Benny hinted, as they got off the bus and headed back to the hotel.

Henry counted his change. "You're in luck, Benny," he said. "I think we have just enough for ice cream."

It wasn't long before they found an ice cream parlor and ducked inside. They soon came out again, happily licking ice cream cones.

"Somebody sure made up hard clues,"

Benny commented, falling into step beside Henry.

Jessie agreed. "This riddle will be a tough one to figure out."

"There's no such thing as flying fish," said Benny, licking a drop of chocolate-mint ice cream from the back of his hand. "Is there?"

"Not exactly." Violet smiled at her little brother. "But sometimes fish leap out of the water."

Henry nodded. "And they almost seem to be flying."

"And the 'bank' in the riddle," put in Jessie, following her brother and sister's train of thought, "could mean the bank of a river or stream."

As they rounded the corner, Violet put up a hand to shade her eyes. "Isn't that Reena coming out of the hotel?"

"Yes, I'm sure of it," said Jessie.

"Hi, kids!" Reena called out. "I just stopped by to see you."

Benny ran forward. "You'll never guess what, Reena," he cried. "I bought a T-shirt with the Space Needle on it!" He held up a shopping bag.

Reena's smiled widened. "Well, maybe you could wear it tomorrow," she suggested. "If you're free, I'd love to show you around the Pike Place Market."

"Sounds great," said Violet. She smiled back at Reena. "We haven't made any plans yet."

"Oh, good!" Reena looked relieved. "The market really is a must-see for visitors. I'm working until noon tomorrow. Why don't I meet you in the hotel lobby around lunchtime?"

"Count us in!" said Henry, and the others nodded.

"Great!" Reena looked down at her wristwatch. "Well, I'm going to be late for work if I don't hurry. See you tomorrow," she said, dashing away.

Jessie stared after her, puzzled. "Reena sure wants to keep us busy," she remarked.

"Oh, Jessie!" said Violet. "You're not still thinking she's trying to distract us, are you?"

"Yes," Jessie answered with a quick nod. "I just don't know why."

"There's no proof Reena's up to anything," Violet insisted, as they stepped into the lobby.

Violet had a point. It was one thing to suspect somebody. It was another thing to have proof.

The important thing right now," said Henry, "is to find out where these clues are leading us."

"You're right, Henry," said Jessie. "With a bit of teamwork, maybe we can figure it out."

* * * * *

"What a perfect day to eat outdoors," Violet said later. She was passing around paper plates and napkins.

"It sure is," said Jessie. "I'm glad Toby mentioned there was a park nearby."

The four Alden children were sitting cross-legged on a blanket spread out on the grass.

"I hope it's a perfect day for solving a mystery," said Benny. He held out his cup as

Jessie poured the lemonade.

"Which one?" asked Henry, as Violet handed him an egg salad sandwich. "The mystery of the riddles? Or the mystery of Rachel?"

"And what about the look-alikes?" put in Benny. "That's kind of weird, too. Don't you think?"

The others had to admit their little brother was right. Violet started adding everything up on her fingers.

"First there was the woman with the umbrella," she said. "The one who bumped into me outside the Hungry Heart Diner."

"She reminded you of Aunt Jane," Jessie recalled.

Violet nodded. "And then there was the snapshot we took on the ferry."

"Right," said Henry. "That man in the photo sure looked like Uncle Andy."

"And don't forget about Mrs. McGregor," added Benny. "She was standing right by the totem pole in Pioneer Square."

Henry smiled at his little brother. "At least

you saw somebody who *looked* like Mrs. McGregor, Benny."

"A lot like Mrs. McGregor," Benny insisted.

Jessie couldn't help giggling. It seemed so funny. "I have a good nickname for Seattle," she said. "The Look-Alike City."

Everyone laughed. Then Henry made a suggestion. "Let's just stick to one mystery at a time."

"I was thinking the same thing," said Violet. "How about if we try to figure out the latest riddle?"

Jessie agreed. "The problem is," she said, "where do we find flying fish?"

Nobody had an answer. They were quiet as they ate their sandwiches and celery sticks. After playing Frisbee, they finally headed back to the hotel. They were each wondering the same thing. Where were the riddles leading them?

* * * * *

"I think we should forget about the mystery for a while," Jessie suggested, the next day while they waited for Reena in the lobby.

Violet agreed. "Let's just enjoy our trip to the market."

"A break might help clear our heads," put in Henry.

"Shake out the cobwebs," said Violet, "as Grandfather would say."

The Aldens had puzzled and puzzled over the strange riddle. But they were still no closer to solving the mystery.

As Reena came into the lobby, she gave the Aldens the thumbs-up sign. "No rain in sight!" she announced.

"Whew!" Benny looked down at the Space Needle on the front of his T-shirt. "I don't want to get my souvenir wet."

"Don't worry, Benny," Reena assured him, as they set off. "Even if it rains, most of the market's under cover."

Inside the crowded marketplace, the children made their way past stall after stall of fruits and vegetables, seafood, and freshly cut flowers. When Reena stopped to buy some peaches, Jessie looked around.

"I've never seen such a big market," she said.

Reena nodded. "It stretches for blocks, Jessie," she said.

The Aldens weaved their way through the crowds, following Reena through a network of stairways, alleys, and courtyards. They discovered all sorts of interesting little shops. They checked out stalls of antiques and handmade crafts and stopped to browse through an open-air exhibit on the history of the market. Suddenly Reena stopped so quickly that Jessie almost bumped right into her.

"Flowers!" Reena snapped her fingers. "I knew there was something I'd forgotten. I was supposed to buy flowers for a special dinner party tonight. Wait here for me."

This got Benny's attention. "What's so special about the party?"

"Benny!" Jessie gave her little brother a warning look. "That's not really any of our business."

Reena laughed. "That's okay, Jessie," she

said. Then she turned to the youngest Alden. "The dinner party's for some wonderful friends, Benny. That's what makes it so special." Then she opened the bag of peaches. "Help yourselves," she said, holding the bag out to them.

Benny didn't need to be asked twice. "Thanks!"

As Reena disappeared in the crowds, the Aldens munched on their peaches. It wasn't long before Benny noticed something.

"Look at that!" He pointed to a life-size statue of a bronze pig. "I guess that's the little piggy who went to market," he joked.

Before the others had a chance to speak, a cheer suddenly went up from a crowd gathered nearby. "I wonder what's going on?" said Jessie.

"Let's check it out," Henry suggested.

Full of curiosity, Jessie, Violet, and Benny followed their older brother.

Benny pinched his nose. "Something smells fishy."

"No wonder," said Henry, when they got

FRESH
HOLIBAY

to the front of the crowd. "Look at all the seafood." He gestured towards the ice-filled counters chock-full of seafood.

A man in shorts and a white T-shirt pointed to a large salmon. "I'll take that one," he said.

"Heave-ho!" the clerk, in fish apron and cap, suddenly shouted out as he flung the salmon high. The crowd let out a cheer when another clerk behind the counter caught the fish in mid-air.

Violet clapped her hands. "That's amazing."

"That salmon must weigh fifteen pounds," said a woman wearing dangly earrings.

Jessie nodded. "No wonder everyone's so impressed."

A man nearby remarked, "They always put on quite a show."

The children watched in amazement as fish after fish flew through the air.

"I think we just found what we were looking for," Henry said.

"What do you mean?" Violet asked him.

Henry looked around at his brother and sisters. "What's the first part of the riddle?"

Jessie began to recite, *"If you catch sight / of fish flying high."*

"Omigosh!" cried Violet, in sudden understanding. "Flying fish!"

"You mean, the riddle was leading us right here?" Benny's face lit up.

"There must be a savings bank somewhere close by," finished Henry. "Let's do some investigating."

Jessie, Henry, Violet, and Benny walked all around, keeping an eye out for a savings bank. But they didn't find any—not even a bank machine.

"I don't get it," said Henry. "According to the riddle, it should be here."

Jessie agreed. "The clues seemed to fit."

"I guess we're on the wrong track again," said Benny. He sounded disappointed.

Violet tried to think of something cheery to say. "While we're waiting for Reena, why don't I take a photo of everyone standing around the bronze pig?"

Nobody had any better ideas, so they walked over to the statue and struck a pose. Violet was about to snap a picture when a woman in a flowered dress approached. Violet waited while the woman dropped some change through a slot in the pig's back.

The woman smiled over at the Aldens. "I just wanted to give Rachel a little something," she said, then hurried away.

Violet slowly lowered her camera. "Did you hear that?" she asked, forgetting all about the photo.

Henry nodded. "Rachel must the pig's name."

"And it's the name Grandfather mentioned on the phone," Benny reminded them. "Do you think it's just a coincidence?"

"I'm not sure," said Jessie, her gaze fixed on the statue. "I guess this is some kind of piggy bank." Then she caught her breath, surprised by her own words.

"Wait a minute!" cried Henry. "Are you thinking what I'm thinking?"

Jessie nodded. "A bank standing nearby!"

"Yippee!" Benny did a little dance. "You were on the right track after all, Henry."

"Maybe," said Henry. "We'll know for sure if we find another clue around here."

The four Aldens examined the piggy bank closely. It wasn't long before Jessie spotted something near the foot of the statue. Crouching down, she reached for some paper folded to the size of a postage stamp.

"I hope I didn't keep you waiting too long," said Reena, coming up behind them. She was holding a bouquet of freshly cut flowers.

"Not at all," said Jessie, getting quickly to her feet. "We didn't mind waiting." She slipped the note into her pocket.

"It gave us a chance to look for clues," Benny blurted out. Then he quickly clamped a hand over his mouth. He'd forgotten they weren't supposed to talk about the mystery.

"I see you've met the market's famous pig," said Reena, as if she hadn't even heard Benny's remark. "All the money from the piggy bank goes to charity," she added.

The children quickened their pace as they walked back to the hotel. They were eager to read the mysterious note tucked into Jessie's pocket.

CHAPTER 10

Surprise!

Henry poured lemonade into four tall glasses. As they gathered around the table in the hotel, Jessie carefully unfolded the sheet of white paper.

"Is it another riddle?" Violet wanted to know.

Jessie nodded and took a sip of lemonade. The ice cubes clinked in her glass. The others inched their chairs closer. They wanted to catch every word.

Jessie cleared her throat, then read aloud:

In the heart of the city
where first it began,
all questions are answered
surrounded by fans.

The children sat in puzzled silence. Jessie was about to say something, but Violet spoke first.

"Pioneer Square!" she cried.

Henry gave Violet a confused look. "What about it, Violet?"

"That's where the city first began, isn't it?"

"That's true, Violet," said Henry. "I suppose Pioneer Square is the heart of the city."

"But the clues could fit the Seattle Center, too," Jessie pointed out.

But Benny wasn't convinced. "What about the rest of the riddle?" he said. "The last part doesn't fit either one of those places."

Jessie had to agree. "There would be plenty of shoppers and tourists in Pioneer Square and the Seattle Center," she realized. "But not fans."

"But there would be fans at a baseball game," Henry said, after a moment's thought. "Especially if the Seattle Mariners are playing."

Jessie was bending over the note again. "Now that you mention it," she said, "this riddle could fit a lot of places."

Benny let out a sigh. "That means we have a whole lot of places to check out."

"I guess we got more than we bargained for on this trip," said Jessie.

Henry nodded. "You can say that again."

Just then, Grandfather came through the door. "Hi, kids!" he said. "How was your trip to the market?"

"We had a great time!" said Violet.

The children took turns telling their grandfather about their outing. Jessie finished by saying, "We were just thinking about getting dinner started, Grandfather."

"Why don't we eat out tonight?" Grandfather suggested. "Maybe we can find a nice restaurant within walking distance."

"The Hungry Heart Diner's just down the street," Henry pointed out.

"Sounds perfect," said Grandfather. "It

would be nice to dress up a bit. What do you think?"

Henry raised an eyebrow. "Just to go to the diner?"

"Sure," said Grandfather. "Why not look our best?"

"Don't worry, Grandfather," Jessie assured him. "We'll change into our good clothes."

Soon enough, the children were ready for their dinner out. Violet was wearing her new jeans and a light sweater. Jessie had changed into a denim skirt and hooded white top. Benny had on his favorite pants with the zippered pockets, and Henry was wearing his most grown-up collared shirt.

"I wonder why Grandfather wanted us to get all fancy," said Benny, patting his neatly combed hair. "What's so special about the Hungry Heart Diner?"

Jessie was smoothing her hood in the hall mirror. "I'm not sure, Benny," she said, shrugging a little.

"The Hungry Heart Diner is special to us," Violet pointed out. "After all, that's where the mystery began."

Jessie suddenly whirled around. A funny look came over her face. Then she clapped her hands.

"That's it!" she exclaimed.

A frown crossed Benny's round face. "What's it?"

"I know the answer to the riddle!"

"We already figured that out, Jessie," Benny reminded her. "It's either Pioneer Square or the Seattle Center."

"Or maybe the ballpark," added Henry.

Jessie shook her head. "I think we got it wrong," she said, her voice rising with excitement. "Remember the first part of the riddle?"

"Sure," said Violet, who had it memorized. *"In the heart of the city / where first it began."*

"What if the riddle wasn't talking about where the city began," said Jessie. She paused for a moment to let them think about it. "Don't you see?" she said at last. "Maybe that wasn't it at all."

Henry looked puzzled. "I'm not following you, Jessie."

"What else could it mean?" asked Violet.

"The mystery!" Jessie told them. "The riddle's telling us to go back to where the mystery first began."

"Of course!" exclaimed Violet. "The 'heart' is the Hungry Heart Diner."

"There's only one problem," said Benny.

"You're thinking about the fans, right?" Violet asked him. And Benny nodded.

Henry thought about this for a moment. "Maybe they use fans at the diner to keep the place cool."

"I don't remember seeing any," said Benny.

"Me, either," said Jessie. "But it's worth checking out."

"What a fine group!" Grandfather said, coming into the room. "I still have a few calls to make. Why don't you go to the diner and get us a table. I'll meet you there shortly."

"Sure, Grandfather," said Henry, and the others nodded.

The children soon hurried on their way. But when they stepped inside the diner, Benny's shoulders slumped.

"Uh-oh," he said. "I don't see any empty tables."

"We might have to wait a while," added Violet.

Just then, a young woman with curly red hair came rushing over. The children recognized her immediately. It was Gwen—the waitress who'd taken their orders the other day.

"I'm afraid we're packed with the dinner crowd right now," she told them. "But I might be able to squeeze you into the back room."

The children kept their eyes peeled for any sign of fans as they followed the waitress past the crowded booths and tables.

"After you," said Gwen, as she opened a door onto a darkened room. "I'll get the light switch."

Jessie looked at Henry. Why were the lights off?

As they stepped into the shadowy room, Gwen flicked a switch and lights blazed.

"SURPRISE!!"

The four Alden children stood frozen to the spot, their mouths opened wide as Watch came bounding over. The little dog jumped up on them, barking happily. Around a table in the middle of the room, familiar faces were beaming at them.

Henry, Jessie, Violet, and Benny stared in speechless wonder as Mrs. McGregor gave them a cheery wave. On either side of her, Aunt Jane and Uncle Andy were all smiles. Finn Evans and Toby Spinner were giving each other high-fives, while Reena was laughing and clapping her hands.

"Is this a surprise party...for us?" Benny asked. He couldn't believe his eyes.

"It sure is," said Grandfather, coming into the room behind them. "A surprise party with all of your biggest fans."

As the children sat down, it slowly began to sink in. "You were behind this mystery," Jessie realized. "Weren't you, Grandfather?"

"It was a team effort, Jessie," Grandfather told her. "Everything was planned before we even got to Seattle."

"Your grandfather thought following clues would be an interesting way to see the sights," put in Mrs. McGregor.

Aunt Jane nodded. "You've solved so many mysteries for so many people," she said, looking at each of the Aldens in turn, "we figured it was time you had a mystery of your very own."

Violet had a question. "Did everybody come all this way just for the surprise party?"

"Well, I had a business trip planned for the Northwest," explained Uncle Andy. "Aunt Jane decided to join me."

Mrs. McGregor put in, "And Watch and I tagged along, too."

"Dogs aren't allowed in the hotel," said Reena, "so my father and I have been looking after Watch."

"No wonder you knew Watch's name," Jessie realized.

"And this must be the dinner party you

were talking about," added Violet, who noticed the vase of fresh flowers on the table.

Reena's eyes were twinkling. "Like I said, Violet, it was a party for some very special friends!"

Something was bothering Benny. "Mrs. McGregor, why did you run away from me?"

"I'm sorry, Benny," Mrs. McGregor apologized. "I just didn't want to ruin the surprise. I never expected to see you in Pioneer Square."

"We thought the underground city was the answer to one of the riddles," explained Jessie. "Only, we were on the wrong track."

Henry turned to Uncle Andy. "And you were on the ferry the other day, weren't you?" guessed Henry.

Uncle Andy nodded. "I had a meeting on Bainbridge Island," he admitted. "But I didn't know you were on the ferry until your grandfather mentioned it later."

Violet turned to her grandfather. "You spotted Uncle Andy when we were getting off the ferry, didn't you?"

"Right."

"That's why you wouldn't let me take a picture," Violet concluded.

"Right again," said Grandfather. "I thought it best to hustle you out of there as fast as I could."

"That was a close call, all right!" Uncle Andy laughed, as the waitress put bowls of salad on the table.

Aunt Jane laughed. "Don't feel bad, Andy. I almost blew it myself."

"What do you mean, Jane?" Mrs. McGregor wondered.

Violet had an answer. "Aunt Jane almost knocked me over coming out of the diner."

"I was on a mission to plant clues," explained Aunt Jane. "Only, I got a late start that morning so I was in a rush. I wasn't watching where I was going."

"You also left the riddle at the Space Needle, right?" put in Jessie. "We saw you getting off the elevator."

Aunt Jane nodded. "I was afraid you might

see me, so I tried to stay hidden under my umbrella."

"Unless I miss my guess," put in Henry, "after you planted the clues, you stopped by the hotel to see grandfather."

"Why, yes," said Aunt Jane, surprised that Henry knew this. "I just wanted to touch base about the mystery and—"

"Guess what?" Benny broke in. "You left your umbrella behind."

"What…?" Aunt Jane slapped a hand against her cheek. "Are you serious?"

Grandfather chuckled. "I couldn't believe my eyes when Violet held it up," he said, swallowing a bite of his salad. "I had to do some pretty fast talking!"

Everybody laughed, including Aunt Jane.

Henry looked over at the desk clerk. "You played a part in this mystery, too. Didn't you, Toby?"

Toby nodded. "I hid the clue by the troll."

"Toby's my cousin," Reena added.

"I had a hunch you knew more than you were letting on," said Henry, as he sprinkled pepper onto his salad.

"I felt someone watching us," said Jessie. "The day we went to see the troll, I mean. It was you, wasn't it, Toby?"

"You found me out, Jessie," he said. "The suspense was starting to get to me. I had to find out if you were on the right track."

Benny nodded in understanding. The youngest Alden didn't like to be kept waiting in suspense either.

Violet spoke up. "We overheard you on the phone, Grandfather, when we got back from Pioneer Square. You said everything depended on finding Rachel."

Grandfather smiled a little. "Oh, you heard that, did you? That must have been when Reena phoned me."

"You were talking about the bronze pig at the market, weren't you?" Violet added.

Grandfather didn't deny it. "Finn was afraid you'd never figure out his clue about the flying fish. He insisted somebody take you on a tour of the marketplace. I'd planned to take you myself, but something came up.

Reena was kind enough to fill in for me."

"I was worried you'd never find Rachel," said Finn. "And solving the mystery depended on it."

The children were looking over at Finn in surprise. You made up the riddles?" Benny questioned.

"There's nothing I like better than a mystery," said Finn. "When your grandfather told me about his plan, I offered to help out."

"You sure did a good job," Benny told him, popping a cherry tomato into his mouth.

Jessie added, "I'll second that!"

As the waitress refilled their water glasses, Henry watched her closely. As if feeling his eyes on her, Gwen looked over.

"Yes, I was in on it, too, Henry," she confessed, reading his mind.

"Gwen's a friend of mine from school," Reena told them. "She wanted to help out."

Gwen explained, "It was my job to make sure you sat down at the right table."

Jessie nodded. That explained why she'd

asked them to move to the booth.

"We saw you one day, Gwen," said Violet. "You were walking with Reena."

"Wow!" Reena shook her head in disbelief. "You kids don't miss a thing."

"Well, we do miss things sometimes," Jessie said, with a twinkle in her eye. "When our trip ends, we're sure going to miss Seattle!"

"And our new friends," Violet was quick to add.

Finn nodded approvingly. "Well said!" he remarked. Then he turned to Grandfather. "You must be very proud of your family, James."

At that, Grandfather had to laugh. "Finn, I never know what's around the next corner."

"I do," Benny piped up. "I bet it's another mystery!"

GERTRUDE CHANDLER WARNER discovered when she was teaching that many readers who like an exciting story could find no books that were both easy and fun to read. She decided to try to meet this need, and her first book, *The Boxcar Children*, quickly proved she had succeeded.

Miss Warner drew on her own experiences to write the mystery. As a child she spent hours watching trains go by on the tracks opposite her family home. She often dreamed about what it would be like to set up housekeeping in a caboose or freight car—the situation the Alden children find themselves in.

While the mystery element is central to each of Miss Warner's books, she never thought of them as strictly juvenile mysteries. She liked to stress the Aldens' independence and resourcefulness and their solid New England devotion to using up and making do. The Aldens go about most of their adventures with as little adult supervision as possible—something else that delights young readers.

Miss Warner lived in Putnam, Connecticut, until her death in 1979. During her lifetime, she received hundreds of letters from girls and boys telling her how much they liked her books.